JACK MARLOWE

TRULY TERRIBLE TALES

INVENTORS

h

Hodder
Children's
Books

a division of Hodder Headline plc

Text © Jack Marlowe 1997
Illustrations © Scoular Anderson 1997

First published in 1997 by Hodder Children's Books

Designed by Don Martin

10 9 8 7 6 5 4 3 2 1

A catalogue record for this book is available from the British Library.

ISBN 0 340 66722 2

Hodder Children's Books
A division of Hodder Headline plc
338 Euston Road
London
NW1 3BH

Printed and bound by Mackays of Chatham plc, Chatham, Kent

Contents

iv

Introduction

Some inventors are brilliant... and sad. They use their great brainpower to invent something, then some soldier comes along and uses their idea to kill other people.

In the early 20th century, the mathematician Albert Einstein worked out that if you could split the tiniest particle of matter - the atom - you'd release a huge

amount of energy. Imagine what a great idea this was. Cheap power from atoms, Einstein thought. But someone else used the discovery first... to make a hugely powerful bomb that killed tens of thousands of people at the end of World War II. Einstein was brilliant ... but sad.

Some inventions can bring misery. Even something as useful as a motor car is accused of poisoning the Earth and killing hundreds of thousands of innocent people.

But other inventions have brought a lot of happiness. In 1997, people were asked, "What is the world's greatest invention?"

What would you have answered? The radio, so we can talk and listen to people on the other side of the world? That was number 6 in the top ten. The wheel was in fifth place and fire was in fourth place. The printing press was number 3 and the computer number 2. So what was number 1?

The toilet!

Who invented this incredibly popular device? And why? Read on to find out...

ARCHIMEDES
287 – 212 BC

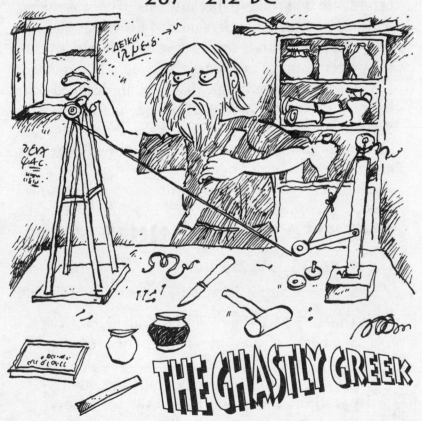

THE GHASTLY GREEK

In Greek times, the greatest mathematician was Archimedes, who lived on the island of Sicily. He had good ideas that he used to build really useful machines. Some of his ideas are still being used today.

But he also used his own ideas to create war machines more terrible than anyone had ever seen before. He built these because his city was being attacked and the defenders needed his clever ideas to help them. Of course, this meant he used his inventing power to make machines that would kill people.

Perhaps it was only fair that Archimedes died violently, just like the victims of his war machines! And the truly terrible story of his death shows that the inventing business can be a dreadfully dangerous one...

THE DEATH-MACHINE MAN

20 AUGUST, 212 BC

The sun had set over the walled city of Syracuse. It was the end of one of the hottest days of the year.

On the top of the city walls the guards paced up and down nervously. Far below them in the harbour, the enemy ships rocked gently. The Romans. There were a few lights showing on the ships, cooking fires and torches, but not much movement. The Romans wouldn't attack tonight.

2

The guards wiped their sweating brows and rested on their spears. The city itself was lit and the sky was bright with stars, but the path below the walls was in deep shadow. Even if the guards had leaned over the walls and peered down, they wouldn't have seen the small door open at the foot of the tower. They wouldn't have seen the man in the dark cloak step out and close the door quietly behind him.

He kept close to the wall and walked quickly to where the path joined the main road to the harbour. There was a chance that he would be seen – a darker shadow on the dark road - but no one would recognise him and no one would be able to stop him.

At last he reached the stone jetty and hurried down some stairs to a small boat, waiting below. He nodded at the Roman soldiers in the boat and they rowed carefully out to a huge galley. Their oars were covered with

rags but the guards on the walls wouldn't have heard them anyway. Carts were trundling through the streets of Syracuse, barrels were being rolled into the taverns and the citizens seemed to be in a carefree mood.

The man from the city climbed on to the galley and a Roman was waiting at the top of the ladder. The Roman was dressed in a cool toga while the men around him were all in armour. He reached out a hand to the man from the city and helped him up the last few steps.

"You received my message, then, General Marcellus?" the man in the brown cloak said. His face was thin and his eyes too close together.

General Marcellus nodded briefly. "Why do you want to betray your city, Philip?" he asked harshly.

The man shrugged. "This siege has gone on nearly three years now. I am starving and I'm tired of being a prisoner in Syracuse. I want an end to the siege. I want you to capture the city and get it over with."

"What else do you want?" Marcellus asked.

The man spread his hands, "If you want to give me a small reward, I would not refuse it."

The Roman general raised one eyebrow.

5

"I'm sure you wouldn't."

He led the way into a cabin on the deck where a red-faced, grey-haired soldier was already seated at a table. "This is my lieutenant, Severus. He will lead the attack."

The lieutenant looked at the spy with disgust. He didn't like traitors, whoever they were working for. "We've tried attacking for over two years now and every time you drive us back. Why should we succeed now?"

Philip looked at him slyly. "We are short of food in Syracuse, but we have plenty of wine. Tomorrow is a festival day and everyone will be drinking – including the guards. By evening they will be too drunk to notice a small band of Romans coming into the south tower door."

"It could be a trap," Severus argued.

"Then I'll come along with you," Philip told him.

"There'll be none of your death machines waiting for us?" General Marcellus asked sharply.

Philip gave a wide grin and showed his small sharp teeth. "Archimedes' toys?"

"They're not toys, they've killed hundreds of Romans in the past two years. Is this Archimedes the inventor?"

"Archimedes is a brilliant mathematician," Philip said. "He doesn't make the machines himself – he hates the idea of being some

sort of mechanic – but he tells us how they can work. He doesn't just make war machines, you know; he has a machine for lifting water uphill."

"What use is that?" Severus sneered.

"It can lift river water onto the fields and keeps our crops watered in the dry season. If we didn't have our Archimedes screws we'd have starved a year ago."

"So he's a Syracuse hero, is he?"

"The people here love him and his funny ways. Did you know he was arrested once for running down the street with no clothes on?"

7

"What happened?"

"Well, it seems old King Hiero had a problem with some money. He thought the goldsmith was trying to cheat him by adding cheap metal to some gold coins. So the king sent for Archimedes and asked him to test the coins. Well, Archimedes used all his clever maths and things for days and couldn't find a way to do it. Then, one day,

EUREKA!

he climbed into the public baths. The tub was full right to the top. When he sat in it the water flowed over the side."

"What has that got to do with testing for gold?"

"The water overflowing gave Archimedes the answer. He decided to drop the suspicious coin in some water and see how much water overflowed. Then he dropped in the same weight of pure gold and saw how much water overflowed. The fake coin spilled more water than the pure gold - so the fake coin wasn't gold! See? He was so excited that he jumped out of the bath and ran down the street shouting 'Eureka'!"

"What's 'Eureka' then? Greek for 'Give me a towel quick'?" Severus asked sourly.

"No. It's Greek for 'I have found it'. Anyway it seems he proved that the coins were a fake. The goldsmith was arrested and executed."

"I wish we had his invention in Rome," the general said quietly.

"And he worked on things called 'levers' and 'pulleys' - they're ropes that run round wheels. He could use them to move huge weights with just one hand. He once used his pulley things to move a sailing ship by himself."

"A useful machine. But it must have been a small ship."

"It was huge. It was the royal ship the Syracusa. It was fully loaded and ready to sail. It should have taken a hundred men to push it into the water. Archimedes did it by himself - well, with the help of his levers and pulleys. Everybody cheered and he turned to the crowd and he spoke. I'll never forget it."

"What did he say?"

"He said, 'Give me somewhere to stand and I will move the Earth!' If he could get to the Moon he'd probably do it as well!"

"And he invented the machines that murdered my men, did he?" Severus asked.

"Well, he designed those huge machines that reached over the walls, grabbed the front of your ships and lifted them up in the air. The people of the city crowded on to the walls to watch that. The great machine shook the ships around a bit till all the sailors fell out and dropped them down till they crashed onto the water and sank! You have to admire his cunning," Philip said.

"Not if you're a drowning sailor you don't," the Roman lieutenant spat furiously.

"Sorry," Philip said quickly. "I was forgetting."

"And my soldiers who died. I suppose this Archimedes invented the catapults that are so much better than ours. They dropped huge boulders on our heads or threw massive logs on top of us every time we marched

Aaggh, no! They've got a catapult!

forward. Those machines had some Romans so scared they just had to see a rope or a piece of wood appear on top of your walls and they turned and ran."

"There are stories about him inventing even more terrible weapons," the spy said.

"They say he has invented huge war-mirrors. The sun will reflect off the mirrors as a really narrow beam of light. And that beam of light will be so hot it'll set fire to anything it touches. He could turn the mirrors on your ships here in the harbour and burn them to ashes!"

Severus's face was turning a deeper red. "He's a dangerous man. I want to be the one to kill him when we get into Syracuse."

"I could lead you to him," Philip said eagerly. "I'm sure that must be worth a little silver."

"No!" General Marcellus said suddenly. "I want that great mind working for Rome. I want Archimedes taken alive and I want him brought to me."

Severus glared at his general. "He has killed hundreds of our men, sir."

"He has not. He has used his skills to defend the people of Syracuse. He can repay us by helping the people of Rome. I want him alive, Severus."

The lieutenant looked away angrily, but muttered, "Yes, General."

The next evening, Severus was at the head of the Roman column that slipped quietly up the path beneath the walls and hurried through the small gateway. Philip was waiting inside and, when Severus had directed officers to different parts of the city, he took his arm and said, "This way to the house of Master Archimedes. He is not interested in jointing the festival."

"Show me," Severus demanded.

"Have you the silver?"

The Roman took a leather pouch from his belt and threw it at the spy. "Now, lead me to Archimedes."

The two men hurried along the walls till they reached a stairway leading down. Guards rested drunkenly against the walls and hardly noticed the two men. The raid on the city was going so quickly and smoothly that the people of Syracuse didn't even know they were being attacked. There was no sign of defenders gathering in the streets.

At last Philip reached a doorway and said, "The house of Archimedes, lieutenant."

Severus did not say 'Thanks' but pushed past him into the hallway. He called, "Archimedes!" There was no answer. "He'd better be here," he said, "or I'll skin you." But when he looked around, the little spy had vanished into the gloom of the Syracuse street.

Now Severus was alone in the house. The man who made death machines might be in here somewhere. He might have machines waiting to destroy unwanted visitors. The Roman drew his sword and crept along the passage that was lit by a single candle. He

13

listened at a door, lifted the latch and pushed it open gently. The room was in darkness.

He climbed the stairs, each step gentle and careful. At the top there was another door and a little light spilled from underneath it. The soldier used his sword to lift the latch at arm's length and push it open. A man in a white tunic was crouched on the floor. He had long, white hair and it hung forward over his face as he

scratched on the floor with a metal instrument.

"Archimedes?"

The man looked up, irritated. "Go away. I am not to be disturbed."

"I am arresting you in the name of Marcellus, Roman conqueror of Syracuse."

"You can see I am busy," the Greek mathematician snapped. "Leave me alone. Get out."

Severus's face was turning purple with rage. "You will come with me."

"Perhaps when I have finished this calculation."

"Now!" The soldier stepped forward and raised his sword.

"I am nearly finished," Archimedes said calmly then turned his back on Severus and continued scratching a diagram in the wood of the floor. "This is more important than your foolish war."

The Roman was breathing fast with harsh breaths. "You have murdered hundreds of my men with your death machines."

Now Archimedes stood up and turned angrily. "Quiet, you stupid man!" he cried.

It was more than Severus could bear. He brought the sword down quickly. It was a stroke from a powerful man who knew exactly how to use the weapon.

The Greek fell towards the floor without a

15

cry and was dead before he hit it.

Severus looked at his sword, wiped it on the dead man's tunic and backed out of the room. "And now," he said softly, "you have made me disobey a direct order from my general. I'll probably die for that. I am your last victim, death-machine man."

THE TRUTH ABOUT ARCHIMEDES

There is no record of what happened to the soldier who killed Archimedes.

Another report of his murder says that Archimedes had some rare instruments that he'd made for his experiments. He was trying to pack them away safely when the soldiers arrived. They thought he was trying to escape with treasure so they killed him.

Whichever story is true, it seems that the man who invented some of the world's cleverest war machines died by one of the world's simplest - a sword.

We are not so sure about the famous stories of Archimedes' inventions. Modern historians say...

the story of the inventor jumping out of the bath and shouting "Eureka!" is probably not true.

the story about giant mirrors being used to set fire to Roman ships is probably untrue because they simply wouldn't work.

Archimedes described the screw for lifting water, so most people thought he invented it. In fact it was being used long before he was born. That story is not true.

BUT the ship-shaking machine seems to have really been built and to have worked. All the stories about the siege of Syracuse mention it. The trouble is that no one quite knows what it looked like.

The Greek history writer Plutarch said this:

The Roman ships were grabbed by machines on the walls of Syracuse. They were whirled about and thrown against the steep rocks that stand below the walls. A ship was often raised to a great height - a dreadful thing to see - and was rolled from side to side. It was kept swinging until the sailors were thrown out then it was smashed against the rocks or dropped.

A Swedish engineer built something that grabbed ships below the water and lifted them up. But that would only work when the ships sailed directly over the top of the machine.

The writers describe something that was operated

from the walls and came from above. It must have been something like a miniature fairground crane that picks up sweets or toys.

The ship smasher may have worked something like this...

THE BOETIAN FLAME-THROWER

In about 400 BC the Greeks of Athens were at war with the Greeks of Boetia. The Boetians invented a weapon that sprayed an oily liquid through a hollow tree trunk and over a flame. The liquid caught fire and was thrown against the enemy walls. When the wooden walls caught fire the defenders would run for cover and the Boetians could enter the city. This was first used at Delium and it worked. The Greeks had the world's first flame-thrower.

It may have looked something like this:

Archimedes wasn't the only inventor to come up with the ancient world's weapons of terror. Here are some other truly terrible weapons from history:

GREEK FIRE In 674 AD the city of Byzantium was surrounded by the armies of Damascus. But the people had a secret weapon. It was invented by a Syrian chemist called Callinicus. He had invented "Greek Fire".

This sticky jelly stuff was sprayed onto enemy ships through tubes. As soon as it squirted through the tubes and mixed with the air it caught fire. The enemy ships burst into flames - and so would any sailors who got in the way! Worst of all, it couldn't be put out with water. The mixture was kept a secret for many years, and even now no one is quite sure what went into it. The people of Byzantium continued to use it for another 800 years until their empire was conquered. By that time the inventors had come up with a new and murderous substance... gunpowder.

GUNPOWDER

In the 1200s, a monk called Roger Bacon wrote down the method of making gunpowder. Many people think he invented it... but he didn't. Some unknown inventor from China had made it hundreds of years before, but he'd used it to make fireworks.

It was another monk, Berthold Schwartz, who first discovered you could use the explosive force to shoot something out of a weapon. It's strange that fun things like fireworks were changed by peaceful men like monks into a weapon that has killed millions and millions of people in history!

Gunpowder often hurt the people using it as much as the people being shot at. King James II of Scotland had the top of his head blown off when his own cannon exploded.

Archimedes wasn't the only weapon user to come to a truly terrible end.

LEONARDO DA VINCI

1452 - 1519

THE DANGEROUS DREAMER

Some inventors are so brilliant they have ideas that are too clever. Leonardo da Vinci invented things that the workers of the Middle Ages couldn't build!

Leonardo was born in Florence, Italy, and had the best teaching there was at the time. Leonardo seems to have been able to do anything. He was a good musician, a fine talker and a wonderful artist.

There is a story that Leonardo's teacher, the artist Andrea del Verrocchio, was working on a large religious painting. Students like Leonardo would often fill in small details that the artist couldn't be bothered to do. Verrocchio asked young Leonardo to paint an angel in one corner. Leonardo's angel was so beautiful that it made Verrocchio's work look plain. The teacher gave up painting because he knew he'd never be as good as his pupil! Verrocchio took up sculpture instead... but that was no escape, because Leonardo turned out to be a wonderful sculptor too!

When he was 30 years old, Leonardo wrote a letter to the Duke of Milan and offered to build him wonderful weapons of war - as well as creating marble, bronze and clay sculptures. The Duke gave him the job. Leonardo became an inventor as well as an artist.

He was always trying something new. The trouble is he wasn't very good at finishing off some of the jobs he started... and some of his new ideas didn't work. He covered a wall with a painting of the Bible story of the Last Supper. Other artists used to paint on to wet plaster so the colour soaked in and stayed for hundreds of years. Leonardo tried to use oil paints - and failed. It took him two years to complete, but the paint started to flake off after just three years.

That failure was sad, but harmless. Some of his other experiments were more dangerous. Leonardo had a student called Zoroastro who suffered more than most from Leonardo's failures. If Zoroastro had written a letter home, then it may have explained the truly terrible problems of working for an inventor like Leonardo...

The suffering student

Palazzo Belvedere
The Vatican
Rome
25 June 1515

Dear Mum,
Sorry I haven't written for a while but I've been a bit poorly. No, don't worry. It's nothing serious, just a little accident. Well, quite a big accident actually, but I'm alive and recovering with just this broken leg. It could have been worse, Mr da Vinci says. He says it could have been a broken neck.

The nuns in the Vatican here are looking after me very well. Mr da Vinci visits me every day and looks at my leg. He says it's healing well. The only trouble is he's got these plans. Plans for things for his new inventions that he wants me to try out. To be honest, Mum, I'm not too keen and I wouldn't mind coming home and working in the butcher shop with Dad. You see, the last invention almost killed me. I'm afraid the next one will.

Songbirds

Mr da Vinci

Me

That's really lovely Mr da Vinci

Jug

Window

orange

Don't get me wrong! Mr da Vinci is a wonderful man. He's a genius with some of the best ideas anyone ever had. The trouble is they don't always work. Especially the last one. He has hundreds of ideas but he has one real favourite. One great dream. He wants to invent a flying machine! The Pope laughed at him and said, "If God had meant us to fly he'd have given us wings!" That's what gave Mr da Vinci the idea. He decided to make some wings.

It all started years ago. He bought birds from the market - you know the song birds that rich people like to keep in their houses. He brought half a dozen home one day and you should have heard them sing. It was really lovely. "That's really lovely, Mr da Vinci," I said.

"Wring their necks," my master said.

"They don't sing so well with broken necks," I said. To be honest, Mum, I thought he was joking. But he was stroking his beard and frowning and he only does that when he's serious.

Well, I had to do as I was told and that was horrible. But what happened next was worse. He started cutting them up! Not just cutting them up but making drawings as he went along. In the end I got the nerve to ask him what he was doing. "Seeing how birds' wings work," he said. "If we can see how a bird flies then maybe we can make a man fly!"

Now Mr da Vinci is getting a bit old. I thought maybe he'd gone a little soft in the head. What I should have thought is, "He's too old to try out a flying machine." But I never suspected a thing.

"See the muscles here?" he'd say. "And look at the shape of the wing. And see these joints?" To be honest I was feeling a bit sick. I don't mind eating the things when they're roasted but all that blood and bones and stuff was a bit much for me.

After a week of drawing and cutting and studying he said, "It's clear a man could never fly by flapping his wings."

Hah! The great Leonardo da Vinci took a whole week to discover that! I could have told him in two seconds! But then he got that dangerous look in his eye, and said, "But I could build a machine using cranks and pulleys and levers so a man can glide on wings like a bat!"

"No one would be daft enough to try it out!" I told him. He just smiled. I should have guessed from that smile that he meant trouble. "What happens if the wings come loose while the flier is in the air?" I asked.

"I've thought of that," he said quickly. He pushed another piece of paper in front of my nose. "The flier would have this device fastened to his back - I call it a parachute. As you can see, the air is trapped in the material and the flier would float to the ground as gently as a dandelion seed."

"Huh," I said. "Dandelion seeds aren't as heavy as a man."

"We'll see," Mr da Vinci said and he went off to his workshop. For the next month I was buying wood and cloth and fine rope. Mr da Vinci began making a huge pair of bat wings. When they were folded they were small but they opened up to fill the room. He fastened the wings to my shoulders. "Just to try them for size," he said. I should have guessed what he was up to, Mum. I should have guessed.

Me with batwings

church

Mr da Vinci's Cat

Last week he announced there would be a demonstration of his flying machine from a tower overlooking the River Tiber. I was really excited. People came from miles around. Of course I was worried that Mr da Vinci would hurt himself, but I was so excited I helped him get ready.

We arrived at the tower before dawn. I carried the wings - they were quite light - and we climbed a hundred stairs. As the sun rose Mr da Vinci began to fasten the wings together and link up the ropes as the crowds began to gather. That's when I had a shocking thought. "Mr da Vinci!" I cried. "You've forgotten to bring your parry flute!"

"Parachute," he said. "The word is parachute."

"Yeah! Well you've forgotten to bring it! Shall I go back and get it?"

"You can't," he said. "That was just a drawing ... a plan. I haven't actually made one."

"So what happens if you fall out of the wings?" I asked.

"I won't be hurt," he said. "Believe me, I will be safe. Completely safe. Now just let me adjust these straps," he said and began fastening the wings on to me the way he'd done in the workshop.

And that's when I started to get worried. People looked up from the gardens below the tower. The river was about fifty metres away

River
Tiber

Me and Mr
da Vinci on
the tower

and Mr da Vinci said the flier would land in the river.

"You could drown in the river," I said. Then I remembered he'd invented something to help a man float in the water. He called it a life jacket. "Shall I go and get your life jacket?" I asked.

"I never made one," he sighed. "Just hold still while I tie this rope to your feet. The life jacket

me flying

was just a drawing, only a plan. Now step onto the edge of the roof," he said.

I stepped forward and a thousand pairs of eyes gazed up at me and everyone cheered. "Try pulling the ropes," he said.

I pulled the ropes and the wings opened. The crowd gasped. "Now," he said, "just step forward."

"I'll fall off the roof," I said.

"No you won't," he laughed. "You'll fly. You'll be the first man in the world to fly. You'll be famous."

"I'll be dead!" I squawked.

"Dead famous," he shrugged as a wind pushed at the wings and made me stumble forward. At least I think it was the wind that pushed me.

The roof of the tower had gone from under my feet and I hung on the wind like a falcon. "I'm flying!" I cried. Then the wind dropped and so did I. "I'm falling!" I screamed. I have a picture in my mind of a hundred faces looking up with open mouths... then rushing to get out of the way. "I knew I should have had one of those perry flutes!" I groaned as the ground hurried towards me. I said all the prayers I know - I said them very fast, you understand. But God is a bit like Mr da Vinci's wings... a bit of a failure. He let me hit the ground.

When I landed it hurt. That's when I fainted and woke up here in the Vatican Hospital.

Now I know my leg is broken, Mum, but that will get better. What I'm worried about is Mr da Vinci. He visits me every day and brings me presents - big, black grapes today. But he's also bringing me new ideas, Mum, and I'm scared. What's going to happen to me when I get out?

On Monday he told me about his plans to make something called an automobile. It will be a bit like a cannon. You'll light the fuse, the gunpowder will explode in the barrel but no cannon-ball will come out. Instead the cannon on wheels will move forward. And I could just tell by the way he looked at me, Mum ... I could tell who is going to be sitting on it when it goes off! These automobile things will never work! Or, if they do, they'll kill anybody who gets in their way.

Monday's invention

Tuesday's invention

On Tuesday he showed me plans for a new ship sinker. It's like a giant drill that will fasten onto the bottom of a boat and bore a hole through to let the water in. I asked how a man could stay under water long enough to make it work and he showed me a plan for something he called a diving suit. The swimmer has a wine skin full of air and he breathes from it while it's underwater. It'll never work! But guess who'll have to try the diving suit! He even invented something called "goggles" so the diver can see under water. He thinks of everything!

On Wednesday he showed me special floats he's invented. You'll wear them on your feet and be able to walk across water. He's not getting me into those things, Mum. At least not until he's made one of those life-jacket things!

On Thursday he invented more terrible weapons. One is a gun with ten barrels that will

Lucia next door →

Wednesday's ← invention

Thursday's invention

"Wham!"

fire ten shots at once. The other is like a crossbow only it's huge. It would fire giant missiles at the enemy. Luckily he never actually builds most of these awful things. But what if he does? And what about if it backfires, I say. Guess who'd be standing there?

On Friday he had a war machine that will go into battle and keep you safe. This armoured chariot will have metal walls and keep enemy bullets out. Guess who'll be inside when he tests it? I wish he'd stick to painting. The nuns here tell me he did a lovely portrait of a lady they call the Mona Lisa. She's smiling and they say everybody wonders what she's smiling at.

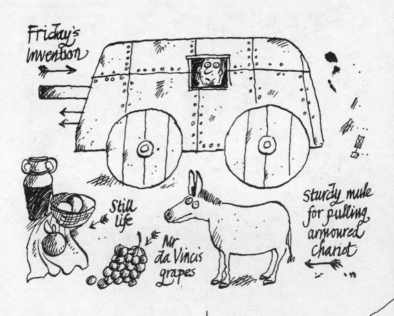

Friday's invention

Still life

Mr da Vinci's grapes

sturdy mule for pulling armoured chariot

I can guess. He's probably telling her the story of me trying to fly. That's enough to make a cat laugh.

They also told me that the Pope Leo X thinks Mr da Vinci is a bit of a failure. "This man will never get anything done," he said. And it's true. Mr da Vinci is always rushing off and trying some new idea before he's finished the last one.

So many ideas! He has plans for draining marshes and building canals, machines for turning meat as it roasts over the fire, plans for making maps and building towns. But none get finished. I only wish he hadn't finished the flying machine! Then my leg wouldn't hurt so much.

The trouble is he keeps his ideas to himself. He draws pictures and writes notes but he

Pope Leo who says Mr da Vinci is a failure

Sister Maria and Sister Dolorosa, the nice nuns at the hospital

View from the hospital window

More grapes from Mr da Vinci

picture of my bandage signed by Mr da Vinci

Leonardo da Vinci

writes them in a strange way. He writes them left handed and back to front so you could only read them if you had a mirror!

He's an amazing man, but I am worried that he is going to kill me if I don't come home soon. Please, Mum, save your suffering son. Let me come home as soon as my leg is better. If God had meant us to fly he wouldn't have given us breakable legs.

Give my love to Dad, to my brothers and sisters.

Zoroastro

Leonardo died at the age of 67, a few years after his stay in Rome. He'd moved to France where the king said proudly, "No man has ever been born in the world who knows as much as Leonardo."

One of Leonardo's last great schemes was for a canal that would link the Atlantic Ocean to the Mediterranean, but as usual it was never built. Anyway, the French were much more amused by one of Leonardo's inventions that did get built. It was a mechanical lion that walked across the floor. Its chest opened to show the coat of arms of the king of France. Just a toy, really, and not the sort of wonderful invention that we should remember him for.

Into the unknown

Aeroplanes first flew less than 100 years ago. But Leonardo's plans were drawn up 500 years ago and the first attempt at flight was probably over 2000 years before that! King Bladud of Britain strapped on feathered wings, jumped off a cliff... and came to a very messy, very sticky death.

It just goes to show, you never can tell when an idea started. But you can try. Here are ten inventions. Can you guess when they were first tried?

* **IN THE ANCIENT TIMES OF GREECE AND ROME**
  (from 1000 BC to 500 AD),

* **IN THE MIDDLE AGES,**
  (from 500 AD to 1500 AD),

* **In Early Modern times**
  (from 1500 to 1840) or

* **In Victorian times**
  (from 1840 to 1900).

Draw a ring around the answer you think is right.

1

**First flight
in a
BALLOON**

✳ ANCIENT

  ✳ ⲙⲓⲆⲆⳑⲉ ⲁⲅⲉⲋ

    ✳ Early Modern

      ✳ Victorian

✳ ANCIENT

  ✳ ⲙⲓⲆⲆⳑⲉ ⲁⲅⲉⲋ

    ✳ Early Modern

      ✳ Victorian

2

**First idea
of a
CAMERA**

3

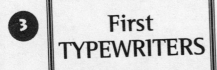

**First
TYPEWRITERS**

✳ ANCIENT

  ✳ ⲙⲓⲆⲆⳑⲉ ⲁⲅⲉⲋ

    ✳ Early Modern

      ✳ Victorian

4

**First
READING
GLASSES**

✳ ANCIENT

  ✳ ⲙⲓⲆⲆⳑⲉ ⲁⲅⲉⲋ

    ✳ Early Modern

      ✳ Victorian

First
POTATO
CRISPS

5

* ANCIENT
  * middle ages
    * Early Modern
      * Victorian

6 The first
LIGHTHOUSE

* ANCIENT
  * middle ages
    * Early Modern
      * Victorian

7

* ANCIENT
  * middle ages
    * Early Modern
      * Victorian

The first
GLASS
MIRRORS

* ANCIENT
  * middle ages
    * Early Modern
      * Victorian

8 The first
CHRISTMAS
CARDS

9

The first
CHEWING
GUM

✳ ANCIENT
　✳ ᴍɪᴅᴅʟᴇ ᴀɢᴇs
　　✳ Early Modern
　　　✳ Victorian

✳ ANCIENT
　✳ ᴍɪᴅᴅʟᴇ ᴀɢᴇs
10　✳ Early Modern
　　　✳ Victorian

The first
TINNED
FOOD

Answers

1 Early Modern

In 1709 a priest showed a working model to the king of Portugal. The hot air balloon rose four metres in the air, then threatened to set fire to the curtains! The servants shot it down. Jacques Charles of France tried a gas balloon in 1783. When it landed in a village the terrified French peasants hacked it to pieces. Later that year, the Montgolfier brothers of France experimented with sending a duck, a sheep and a hen up in a balloon, before sending François Pilatre into the air. The world's first flier - unless you count King Bladud and Zoroastro!

2 ANCIENT

The Greeks knew that if you shut light out of a room then let in a pin-prick of light, the picture of the outside world will be projected on to a wall. They used this trick to let light fall on a sheet of parchment so they could trace around it and make a drawing. The first photograph was not possible till film had been invented in 1827. The idea for the camera was much, much older.

3 Early Modern

The Italian nobleman Pellegrino Turri had a blind friend, Countess Carolina Fantoni. In 1808 he built a writing machine for her so she could write to him. Some of her letters are still preserved in Italy and one is fifteen pages long. It worked!

4 MIDDLE AGES

A man called Armati of Florence was making glasses around 1290 AD though no one knows who actually invented them. They clipped on the end of the nose and it was another 400 years before Londoner Edward Scarlett invented the side pieces that slide over your ears.

5 VICTORIAN

George Crum was a chef in a United States restaurant. In 1853 a customer complained that his fried potatoes were too thick, so George sliced them wafer thin, fried them and served them They were an instant success. But imagine eating hot crisps!

6 ANCIENT

The first lighthouse was about 130 metres high and was lit by a huge wooden fire in a cage at the top. Imagine climbing all that way to put more wood on! It was on the island of Pharos at the mouth of Egypt's River Nile and was known as one of the Seven Wonders of the World. It was built in 285 BC and lasted till 1302 AD when an earthquake destroyed it. The inventor was said to be King Ptolemy II of Egypt.

7 MIDDLE AGES

In 1279 a monk called John Peckham described a glass mirror. He didn't invent it. Rich Greeks and Romans had used polished silver plates to look at themselves. Poor people looked in the village pond on a calm day!

That'll teach you to look too closely at your spots!

8 VICTORIAN

In 1843 the artist John Calcott designed the first Christmas card for Sir Henry Cole. The card showed a family raising their glasses to wish the reader a Happy Christmas. Several people said this was disgraceful because it encouraged drunkenness! A thousand were printed - now it is millions! Before that date people simply used to write to their friends at Christmas.

9 VICTORIAN

John Curtis of Maine, USA, started making chewing gum in his kitchen in 1848. Which delicious flavour would you have chosen? Sugar cream, White Mountain, Four-in-hand, Biggest and Best or Liquorice Lulu? It was so popular he had to move to a factory two years later. Then he started making new flavours like American Flag. Imagine being asked if you want to chew a piece of American Flag!

10 Early Modern

An English manu-facturer called Bryan Donkin first put food in cans in 1811. He put beef in cans and sent a free sample to the royal family who wrote back and said how much they enjoyed it. But where on earth did they get the can opener from?

Scores

0 - 2 Truly terrible. Maybe someone should invent a brain for you.

3 - 5 There's hope for you... but not much.

6 - 8 You aren't as stupid as you look!

9 Genius!

10 Cheat!

SIR JOHN HARINGTON

1561–1612

TOILETS AND TROUBLE!

Some inventors, like Leonardo da Vinci, are remembered even though most of their inventions didn't work. Some inventors are forgotten even when their inventions are a great success - inventors like Sir John Harington.

Sir John was born into an upper class family. When he was christened Queen Elizabeth I was his godmother. (Elizabeth was known as The Faery Queene so Sir John is probably the only inventor to have had a fairy godmother!)

Some inventions are made to solve a problem. In 1903, for example, Albert Parkhouse was working in a wire factory making frames for lampshades. When he came back from lunch one day he found all the coat pegs had been used up and there was nowhere to put his coat. He snatched up a piece of his wire, bent it into the shape of a coathanger and twisted a hook on the top. He'd invented the world's first wire coathanger and now billions of people use them. (His boss saw the hanger, copied it and started manufacturing wire coathangers. The man made a lot of money from this - Albert Parkhouse got nothing!)

Sir John Harington's invention certainly solved a problem of the time but he didn't invent it simply because it was needed. He invented it because it got him out of trouble!

What did he invent? Something you use several times a day. If Sir John had kept a diary, this is what he might have written...

The queen's nose

3 January 1584

The queen's nose is a very fine nose. A wonderful nose and a beautiful nose. But it is so sensitive, I think she could smell a rotten egg from a mile away. And bad smells upset her. They upset her terribly. And when Elizabeth is upset she makes sure someone else is upset. The queen can be very cruel at times.

I am the same as every other person at court. I tremble to think of what her majesty may say or do next. Last week I wore a new jerkin for the Christmas festival at court. My knees were shaking as I walked into the court. The queen looked at me and said, "It is well cut, Sir John!" She liked it! I breathed again, a happy man.

But then she spied Sir Richard in a new doublet with tassels on and said, "Your mind is like your doublet - it has gone to rags!" Sir Richard made the big mistake of trying to explain that the tassels were for decoration, they were not ragged edges. Her majesty walked up to him and spat on the new clothes. We have not seen Sir Richard in court since that day.

And she hates long cloaks that come down to below the knee. Men who wear long cloaks cannot carry a sword. And she wants the men around her to carry swords to defend her if she is ever attacked. I have even heard her say she is going to pass a law that will ban long cloaks! Back in 1571 she passed a law that said all common men and married women were to wear woollen hats so the wool trade in England would be a success. Whatever next? Perhaps she'll be telling us to blow our noses on yellow handkerchiefs with pink spots!

And, talking of noses (which I was), the queen's fine nose has claimed another victim. Today the Welsh soldier, Sir Roger Williams, was allowed to meet her to ask for a favour. The truth is she did not feel like granting the favour. She was in one of her dark and miserable moods. When she gets like that she looks for any excuse not to speak to someone. Poor Sir Roger came into the room and knelt in front of the queen. Suddenly she leans back in her chair, clutches a hand to her mouth and cries, "Faugh! Williams! I pray you, begone! Your boots stink!"

The poor man rose to his feet, shrugged and walked away saying, "I think you are wrong, madam. It's my suit that stinks!"

I doubt if we'll see Williams at court for a long time. What a dreadful thing, to be banned from the royal palace.

27 May 1584

The queen is such a fussy person. She enjoys being clean. Her ladies say she takes four baths every year whether she needs them or not! She has a bathroom at each of her palaces and she even has a bath that she takes with her when she travels around the country.

Of course the queen is famous for her travels. Every year she sets off with an army of servants and guards and cooks and entertainers and descends upon the home of some poor lord. The lord is then expected to entertain the queen for the summer months when London becomes too hot and smelly and full of the fear of the Plague.

Some people say Elizabeth is restless and cannot stay in one place for long. Some say she loves her people and wants to travel the country and be seen by all of her loyal subjects. Some say she is too mean to pay the bills for all her servants - she moves into some rich lord's home and lets him pay the bills for a month or so. There is a little truth in all of these things. But the real truth is in her nose. She is driven from place to place by the smell.

All the people around her produce a lot of human waste. Of course they use the toilets - or the jakes as the men usually call them. But these toilets soon fill up. After a few weeks in a house the stench is terrible. All the queen can do is move to another house. Soon that is filled with the awful smell of the reeking jakes and she moves on again. Nowhere stays sweet-smelling for long. It doesn't matter how much servants scrub and wash, how many times the jakes are emptied or how deep the pits that hold the waste, the stink is always there. Here at Hampton Court the waste is emptied into drains that run into the

River Thames. Yet the drains smell dreadfully in summer, which is why the queen moves off to the fresh air of the country.

Of course the queen herself uses a lidded stool to relieve herself. She lifts the lid so she can pee into the pot below then puts the lid back down. None of her ladies in waiting enjoy the job of emptying the pot but someone has to do it. Otherwise the lidded stool begins to stink the room out.

Mind you, this is not so foul as the servants here who don't bother with lidded stools. They simply use the palace courtyard.

Summer is coming and the queen will be travelling somewhere again. Many of her older servants hate the journey. The rough roads we have to travel on. The long days in the saddle. The rough beds they have to use in the country and the hard work they must do to keep the queen dressed and fed and entertained. There are a lot of miserable faces around the court this week. They are all hoping that Her Majesty will leave them behind!

3 June 1584

The queen's nose has claimed another victim! The country is run by her nose. The queen has the only running nose in the country! Hah! I'd better not say that to her for she can be very stern with people who make jokes that she disapproves of. After all, I don't want to be banished from the court like the French Ambassador. And what was the poor man's crime? He has stinking breath! As he left the room she exclaimed, "Good God! What shall I do if the man stays here? For I can smell him an hour after he is gone!"

Some cruel person (not I) passed on the queen's complaint to him. He was so embarrassed they say he has packed his bags and gone back to France, never to return. Poor fellow.

The queen herself is quite particular about her breath. She uses tooth cloths to keep her teeth clean and also uses tooth picks to remove meat from between the teeth. Some people give her tooth picks made of gold and studded with jewels as presents at New Year. Sadly I notice that the queen's teeth are turning black and rotten anyway. I have noticed that this often happens to people who eat a lot of sweet foods. Her Majesty's favourite is marzipan and her favourite treat is to eat a chess-board made from the sweet stuff. I believe this may be causing her teeth to rot. Also she is too cowardly to have the bad teeth pulled out when they do rot.

But enough about the queen's teeth. As I said, her nose runs the country. Just eight years ago the queen made an angry speech about the smell of London air in winter when factories and houses burn sea coal. The bitter smoke offends her nose. The brewers of beer in London offered to go back to burning wood! Wood is more expensive because people have been cutting trees to burn the wood or build their houses and ships for hundreds of years. Trees around London are disappearing quickly. Wood needs to be brought a long way over rough roads now to feed the fires. Coal was better - shiploads from Newcastle landed at the docks in the heart of London.

Trees die and men are driven to France because of the queen's nose.

17 October 1584

Disaster. I am banished from court. My baggage cart is packed and I am to return to the west country, Somerset, where I was born.

I am the latest victim of the queen's cruel temper. It was all so silly. Sir Andrew came to court and told a joke about a woman. I took the joke and said the woman was the queen's chief lady-in-waiting.

It was a very rude joke, I must admit, about the lady and the jakes. I will not repeat it here because it is something I want to forget. But Her Majesty came to hear about the joke and she did not laugh. She did not smile. She simply rose to her feet and said in a low voice, "Who is responsible for this foul jest?"

Would you believe it? Everyone turned and looked towards me! What else could I do but confess!

The queen told me that I may enjoy a holiday in the country. A very, very long holiday. Then she turned away from me and acted as if I didn't exist. I may as well go. Oh, cursed be this joking tongue of mine.

30 July 1589

It's been almost five years since I left the queen's court but I have not wasted the time. I have never stopped planning and plotting to win my way back into the heart of my godmother. Now my plans are almost complete.

My father had some land close by the city of Bath and he gave it to me to build a house. I built Kelston Hall over the past four years but I built it cunningly with the queen in mind… or rather the queen's nose.

The queen, as I may have said before, has a very fine nose. Her tours around the country are like a flock of crows. They descend on some nest and when it is totally fouled they fly off to another nest.

I decided that what I needed was to build a system of jakes that are so clean they will be a wonder to her eyes and to her fine nose. So I have built a new type of toilet into the house. There is a tank of water above the toilet. The user sits on the seat and pees (or whatever) into fresh water. The user then pulls a handle on the seat and fresh water rushes down from the tank and flushes out the dirty water. The dirty water is then sent into a large underground pit. There is still a problem of a smell rising from the pit and the thing will have to be emptied every year. But the jakes themselves will smell cleaner than the queen's nose has ever known.

I call my invention Ajax because I have built 'a jakes'! Word will soon reach Her Majesty's ears which are as sharp as her nose. Then she will want to visit Kelston. You'll see.

23 August 1591

It is over. After the years of work and planning Elizabeth has forgiven me and invited me back to her court in London.

The queen's household left Kelston today with her praises ringing through every room, but especially the jakes! They say Ajax was a great hero in ancient Greece. Well, my Ajax has proved to be my hero.

The queen loves my toilets so much she has invited me back to London to build my flushing machines into her palaces.

I am forgiven! They say the way to a man's heart is through his stomach. I can tell you, the way to a queen's heart is through her nose!

17 February 1596

Today is a proud day for me. My book on Ajax is published. It describes how the flushing toilet works and has illustrations to show the clever design.

I had hoped that I would be remembered as a great lord at Elizabeth's court. It seems that instead I will be remembered as the man who gave the world the cleaner toilet. That is something I would be proud to have carved on my gravestone.

In fact Sir John's invention never became popular in his lifetime. The flushing toilet was a brilliant invention but it needed a good drain system with proper sewers to make it really clean and healthy.

Elizabeth was England's first monarch to have a flushing toilet, but it was another two hundred years before the idea really caught on.

TRULY TERRIBLE TOILETS

Have you ever noticed that people in history books never seem to go to the toilet? In fact they did. They were very open about it and not at all ashamed. But over the past hundred years or so it has become a very secret sort of thing to do. So now people don't talk about it and they hardly ever mention it in history lessons.

In fact the history of the toilet is quite interesting. It makes you realise just how lucky you are to live in the twentieth century. Here's a quick look at the story...

1 Historians have dug up ruins of Ancient Crete palaces that have sewers and seem to have toilets with water running through them.

2 The Romans built wide drains to carry heavy rain away from the towns into the rivers. They dumped rubbish in these so they were like sewers and the towns were fairly healthy... but the rivers weren't!

3 The Roman toilets were places to go and meet your friends for a chat. One public toilet dug up near Rome had twenty seats, side by side. The seats were marble. Brrrr! The Romans used sponges dipped in running water instead of toilet paper.

4 In the Middle Ages the monks built their toilets over a water supply. The people of large towns, though, had to make do with toilets on bridges. London Bridge had a toilet that served 100 houses. Everything dropped into the River Thames below. Very messy if you were trying to sail a boat under the bridge!

5 Castles had toilets called garderobes where the waste dropped into the moat outside. Very nasty if you wanted to swim across it to attack the castle, and smelly in summer. Even messier if you were a poor reader and went into a wardrobe instead of a garderobe!

From 1500 to about 1750 toilets became less healthy. People tended to use a chamber pot or the sort of "close stool" described by Sir John Harington. The servants had the unpleasant job of emptying these. The pots were often emptied into the street straight from a window. In Paris a student threw a full pot over the king of France who was riding below the window. The king forgave him... maybe he was a little potty.

In the 18th and 19th Centuries poor people had "privies" at the back of the house. They were just a wooden seat over a pit filled with the dead ashes from the fire. Men called "night soil men" shovelled the ashes and the waste onto carts and carried it away to dump it in deep holes. Unfortunately some of these deep holes leaked the waste into the drinking water and many people in the towns died.

8 Rich people couldn't be bothered to go outside to the privies so they continued to use the chamber pots under the beds and expected the servants to clean them every morning. Some servants were advised to carry the full pots right through the house so everyone could see the mess and even answer the door with a full chamber pot in the hand if someone knocked. This would shame the rich men and women into going outside like everyone else! Some chamber pots had comic pictures or rude comments printed on. They are worth a lot of money now and antique lovers often collect them!

9 In 1775 a watchmaker called Alexander Cumming invented a flushing toilet very similar to Sir John Harington's. This "water closet" became popular and over the next two hundred years most houses were fitted with them. But there were still problems. The pipe that carried the waste from the toilet to the pit could become cracked and leak. Queen Victoria's pipe leaked, and the foul water got into the drinking water used by her husband, Prince Albert. It gave him the disease that killed him.

10 The modern oval shaped toilet bowl was first made by a company called Jennings in 1884. The first public toilets were built in 1852 in London. The owners charged people two pence to use the toilets, which were meant to make money. But in the first year only 82 people paid to use them. In 1855 London Council built toilets for the public and charged just one penny. The price didn't change for over 100 years until decimal currency was introduced in 1971.

What an outrageous price!

PUBLIC TOILETS
CHARGE 2 PENCE

SIR
JOSEPH
LISTER

1827 - 1912

THE CLEAN CUTTER

They are so small you can't even see them. But they can kill you. In fact every second of every day they are trying to kill you! If you're not careful they probably will.

Forget Alien invaders or mad axemen. Our most truly terrible enemies are germs. For thousands of years they won the war with human beings. They killed millions of people. Why? Because human beings didn't even know they were there.

Scruffy doctors tried to cure patients, but in fact they helped to kill them. They were carrying the deadly enemies: germs.

In the war between germs and humans, the germs won every battle. Then a chemist called Louis Pasteur discovered the little terrors. He began treating patients with diseases and curing them.

But surgery was another matter. Surgery is where a doctor cuts open a patient to operate on a faulty part of the body. Patients in surgery were surviving the cutting, but dying when the cuts went rotten and poisoned the blood. English surgeon Joseph Lister read about Pasteur's work and invented ways of cutting people open, stitching them up and keeping them alive.

For the first time ever, the germs were really under threat. If the germs had their own newspaper, then Joseph Lister must have made headlines!

THE INVISIBLE ENEMY

London, 1877

"My mum's scared," the little girl said. She sat on a chair in the hospital corridor. Her legs were covered in dirty white stockings and too short to reach the floor. Her faded cotton dress was crusted with food.

The doctor stopped and looked down at her. "What's your mum scared of?" he asked.

"Dying. She says Mrs Mulligan down the street came to this hospital last year and she never came out alive. She says they're all butchers in this hospital."

"I'm not a butcher," the man said gently and sat down beside her. "I'm Doctor Lister."

"What's your first name?" the child asked.

"Joseph."

"I've got an uncle called Joseph," she said, turning her wide blue eyes on the man in the black suit. "I call him Uncle Joe."

"I see. You must be Lizzie Best, are you?"

"How do you know that?" the girl asked and wiped her nose on her sleeve. The doctor took a handkerchief from his pocket and wiped it for her. "Thanks Mister Joe."

"I am your mother's butcher."

"You really? You going to kill her?"

"I hope not," he smiled.

"What are you going to do?"

"I've looked at her knee where she fell down the steps and her knee cap is broken. The knee cap is the loose bit of bone on the knee."

"I've got one of them!" the girl said.

"Really? I've got two! One on each leg," the doctor grinned.

Lizzie scowled at him. "You know what I mean."

"I do. Now, because that knee cap got broken

your mum isn't be able to walk. And it won't heal up all by itself. I have to open up the skin and fix some wire onto your mum's knee-cap to stop it coming apart again."

"It'll hurt!" the girl said. "She won't half scream!"

Lister shook his head. "She'll be asleep."

"What if she wakes up when you cut her?"

"I mean we'll send her to sleep. We'll give her something called chloroform. It'll put her to sleep and when she wakes up it will be all wired up and stitched together again."

Lizzie nodded and sniffed. "My mum reckons Mrs Higgins gave her a push. That's why she fell down the stairs. Mrs Higgins is our deadly enemy."

The doctor sighed. "I've got enemies."

"Go on, you haven't! Who?"

"Well, I've got big enemies and little enemies. The big ones are the clever doctors who don't want me to do this operation for a start. They say it's too dangerous. The knee cap may be fixed, they say, but the knee will turn bad and put poison in the blood. My big enemies say it would be better to let your mum be crippled all her life rather than die from my operation."

Lizzie was young but she was bright. She nodded wisely and said nothing. Doctor Lister leaned towards her and spoke in a whisper. "But I've got even more deadly enemies than the clever doctors. I've got little enemies called

'germs'. And they are terrible, terrible things
because they're invisible!"

The girl looked up and down the corridor.
She couldn't see anywhere for an enemy to hide.
Then she remembered 'invisible' meant you
couldn't see them anyway. "So how do you know
they're there?"

Doctor Lister explained. "A clever doctor
called Pasteur found them. He says they are so
tiny you can't see them, but they live on dirt. If

the dirt gets into a cut then it carries the germs with it. Then the germs attack your body."

"That's all right, though. If they're that tiny they can't hurt me," Lizzie argued.

"They can if there are millions and millions of them. They can kill you."

Lizzie frowned. "I can't believe it."

"You're not the only one. There are a lot of great doctors who don't believe it either. They think I'm a fool and they laugh at me too."

"So, the great doctors are your big enemies, are they?"

"They are. And because they are stupid and refuse to listen they're as dangerous as my little germ enemies! They keep on operating on people and letting the little germs in."

"And you think your little germ enemies will get my mum?" she asked.

"I hope not. You see, I've found a way of killing those germs off before they even get to a patient. I kill them off with some stuff called carbolic acid. I invented a spray that will fill the room where we operate. I wash all our sharp knives in carbolic acid and I even make sure the nurses and doctors wash their hands in it."

"Those little germs must hate you," Lizzie said.

Doctor Lister rose to his feet. Mrs Best was being wheeled down the corridor towards them.

"And the little germs must love you, Lizzie!"

"What you mean?"

"I mean, I need you as clean as one of my knives when you get your mum home. Do you understand? Clean clothes, clean bed and a clean house. I'll do my best to fight the germs in the hospital. Will you try to fight them in your home?"

"You haven't seen our house!" Lizzie cried.

Doctor Lister had seen her street. It was in the worst slum area of London. His little ene-

mies had been at home there for hundreds of years. They'd win a lot more battles before humans started to win the war.

"Your mum will have her knee mended and be awake in about an hour, Lizzie. You can come and see her then."

He followed the trolley into the operating room and closed the doors behind him. The stinging scent of the carbolic acid spray reached the little girl's nose a few minutes later.

Lizzie looked at the dirt that was ground into her hands and smeared over her dress. She shuddered at the thought of the invisible enemies that were crawling all over her.

"You're not going to get my mum," she said, speaking to a specially nasty grease spot on her cuff. "I'll wash you in that carbolic acid stuff and you'll have to go somewhere else." Suddenly her face brightened into a smile. "You can go and live with Mrs Higgins. You'll love her – and it'll serve her right for pushing my mum!"

Joseph Lister's patient with the wired knee-cap operation recovered completely. The doctors who had laughed at his idea of 'antiseptic surgery' at last began to take him seriously and copy his methods.

Life was going to be much harder for the invisible little enemies in future.

GERM JOURNAL

9 September 1875   Price **3d**

GERMS SQUIRM!

by Bacillus X, our Medical correspondent

FILTHY HUMANS FIGHT BACK

Germs in Britain are in mourning today as millions died in a dreadful attack by mass murderer, the human being Joseph Lister. When we Germ People were discovered by French doc, Louis Pasteur, we guessed it was just a matter of time before humans found ways to destroy us. Now the Germ People's worst nightmare has come true and our civilisation is being wiped out by lousy Lister.

In the past, doctors have been our friends. They gave patients useless medicines and failed to spot us. But our greatest allies have been their super surgeons - the blood-spilling barbers as we call them.

JOSEPH LISTER, PUBLIC ENEMY No. 1.

As we all know, human bodies have natural defences against us. Their blood has the dreaded antibodies that can kill a careless Germ. The more healthy blood a human has then the less chance we have of killing him or her. What did the stupid human doctors do? They tried to cure sickness by draining off the patient's blood! They were too stupid to realise they were weakening the patients and letting us get on with winning the battle.

What will happen now? Germs will be driven out of the operating theatres of the world. Germ People in hospitals are an endangered species. They could become extinct one day. Something must be done before this truly terrible end arrives. Our warrior germs are out to get Lister. The trouble is he is so clean it is proving difficult to get at him.

This is a sad day in the history of Germ Warfare. Those evil humans have turned the tide and Germ People are on the run. Humans who listen to Lister have the power to destroy us. The only ones who can save us are the humans who don't believe him. We must trust that they stay just the way they are - stupid, dirty and careless. Those are the only humans we'll get in future.

Our history correspondent writes:

The greatest era for the Germ People was, of course, the 1340s and 1350s when our

THE BLACK DEATH – OUR FINEST HOUR!

82

Black Death warriors swept across the world and wiped out almost half of the humans on it. We were helped by their ignorance. They didn't know about us then. They didn't even have the sense to work out that we lived in the fleas that hopped from rats to humans and carried us with them.

We have brought some wonderful deaths and diseases including great cholera epidemics, sweating sicknesses, influenzas and dysentery. Without the Germ People these humans would live for much longer and the world would be overcrowded. Now that they've discovered us, and the good we do, they should love us not massacre us.

But history has shown that the Germ warriors are hard to beat. Just when the humans think they've wiped out one deadly disease, we can usually come up with something new they haven't thought about. Our dream is that one day we will come up with a disease they can't cure. One day we will. History is never wrong.

Germ warfare...

What do you know about germ warfare? Try the following questions and see how you do...

True or False?

This might hurt.

On a battlefield a surgeon would try to clean and seal a bullet wound by pouring hot oil into it.

True/false?

2

Surgeons cut off limbs and burned the stump to stop it bleeding until a Frenchman called Ambroise Paré came along. In the 1500s he learned how to tie the ends of blood vessels.

True/false?

Patients liked surgeons with dirty coats. They thought it meant he had done a lot of operations and he must be good.

True/false?

3

4

Joseph Lister wanted clean air in the operating room so he sprayed the air with carbolic acid while he worked.

True/false?

Oh, dearest, I forgot to tell you that I borrowed your...

5

Lister worked in a Glasgow hospital where there were extra problems because it was built over an old graveyard for victims of the deadly cholera disease.

True/false?

Lister experimented on live animals and Queen Victoria tried to stop him.
True/false?

6

We have admired your stitching.

Answers

1 True. But battlefields were dirty places and victims often died from their wounds. Others were beyond help. Ambroise Paré the surgeon described one truly terrible scene:

> We entered the city and found four dead soldiers and three wounded men propped against a wall. They could not see, hear or speak and their clothes were still smouldering. I was looking at them, full

of pity, when an old soldier asked me if I could cure them. I said I couldn't so he went up to them and cut their throats gently and with no hatred.

2 True. Paré also made artificial legs and arms for his patients. But Lister discovered that the silk ties could carry germs. Lister began using thread made from cat-gut.

3 True. They did not wear special gowns for operating as they do today. Surgeons wore ordinary coats that were too old to wear in the street and caked with old blood.

4 True. At first. He sprayed the stuff through a ladies' scent bottle, but the carbolic acid got in the eyes of the doctors and nurses and irritated them terribly. In the end he had to give up this idea.

5 True.

6 True. He experimented on calves and proved that catgut stitches were better in a wound than silk thread. Queen Victoria must have forgiven him because he later operated on her, and she gave him a knighthood - the first to be given to a doctor. He boasted, "I am the only man ever to have stuck a knife into the queen!"

Joseph Lister died when he was 85. He'd kept those germs waiting a long time before they finally got him.

TRULY TERRIBLE TALES

WRITERS

So you think being a writer is a nice, peaceful existence? Think again! This book delves into the action-packed lives and dramatic deaths of writers through the ages.

SCIENTISTS

If you think today's scientists are eccentric, wait till you find out about the dotty and dangerous ideas of four boffins from the past!

EXPLORERS

What makes someone risk everything to sail off into the unknown? Find out by reading the amazing stories of four real-life adventurers.

ORDER FORM

0 340 66724 9	Truly Terrible Tales: Writers	£3.99	☐
0 340 66722 2	Truly Terrible Tales: Inventors	£3.99	☐
0 340 66723 0	Truly Terrible Tales: Scientists	£3.99	☐
0 340 66721 4	Truly Terrible Tales: Explorers	£3.99	☐

All Hodder Children's Books are available at your local bookshop or newsagent, or can be ordered direct from the publisher. Just tick the titles you want and fill in the form below. Prices and availability are subject to change without notice.

Hodder Children's Books Cash Sales Dept
Bookpoint, 39 Milton Park, Abingdon, Oxon OX14 4TD, UK

If you have a credit card, you may order by telephone on (01235) 831700

Please enclose a cheque or postal order made payable to Bookpoint Ltd to the value of the cover price, plus the following for postage and packing:

UK and BFPO: £1.00 for the first book, 50p for the second book, and 30p for each additional book ordered up to a maximum charge of £3.00. Overseas and Eire: £2.00 for the first book, £1.00 for the second book, and 50p for each additional book.

Name ....

Address ....

....

If you would prefer to pay by credit card, please complete:
Please debit my Visa / Access / Diner's Card / American Express (delete as applicable) card number:

Signature ....

Expiry date ....